AMBER

THE STORY OF A RED FOX

SHIRLEY WOODS

ILLUSTRATED BY CELIA GODKIN

ıry & W

www.fitzhenry.ca   godwit@fitzhenry.ca.

10 9 8 7 6 5 4 3 2

National Library of Canada Cataloguing in Publication Data
Woods, Shirley E.
Amber : the story of a red fox / by Shirley Woods ; illustrations by Celia Godkin.
ISBN 1-55041-811-4 (bound).—ISBN 1-55041-810-6 (pbk.)
1. Foxes—Juvenile fiction.   I. Godkin, Celia II. Title.
PS8595.O652A74 2003   jC813'.54   C2003-902338-9
PZ7

U.S. Publisher Cataloging-in-Publication Data (Library of Congress Standards)
Woods, Shirley.
Amber: the story of a red fox / Shirley Woods; illustrated by Celia Godkin. – 1st ed.
[96] p. : ill. ; cm.
Summary: The story of a young fox, from her first month to an independent life.
ISBN 1-55041-811-4
ISBN 1-55041-810-6 (pbk.)
1. Foxes – Fiction. – Juvenile literature. (1. Foxes – Fiction.) I. Godkin, Cecilia. II. Title.
[Fic] 21   PZ7.W6637Am   2003

Fitzhenry & Whiteside acknowledges with thanks the Canada Council for the Arts, the Government of Canada through the Book Publishing Industry Development Program (BPIDP), the Ontario Arts Council and the Government of Ontario through the Ontario Media Development Corporation's Ontario Book Initiative for their support for our publishing program.

Design by Blair Kerrigan/Glyphics
Printed in Canada

For Sandrea,
who loves animals, especially foxes

Author's Acknowledgements

Many people, including the staff of the Bridgewater Library, have helped me in my research for this book.

I am especially indebted to Bob Bancroft for his knowledgeable answers to a wide variety of questions. Wayne Downey has also provided some interesting fox anecdotes. And I am most grateful to Donald Troop for sharing his insights into the behavior of red foxes.

Once again, Celia Godkin has taken great pains to ensure that her fine artwork compliments the story.

Finally, I would like to thank Ann Featherstone for doing all those things that an editor is meant to do — and more.

CHAPTER ONE

A FOX IS BORN

It began to snow just before dawn. The fox paused in mid-stride and glanced up at the dark sky. Snowflakes were floating down like white feathers. A cold flake landed on his pointed nose. Except for a twitch of his long black whiskers, he ignored it. April snow flurries were to be expected on the north shore of Lake Huron.

The fox's mind was on food. He'd hunted the fields all night and had only caught a mouse. Confident that he would find larger prey, he'd eaten the mouse. Soon it would be light, and he had nothing to bring home to his mate. Before giving up the hunt, he decided to try the edge of the forest.

He knew that many small animals lived in the brush and weeds bordering the forest. When he reached the edge of the woods, he stopped to listen and to sniff the breeze. Then he weaved his way through the cover, leaving his footprints like a string of dots in the new-fallen snow.

Presently he came upon the trail of a snowshoe hare. He sniffed the tracks and found they were fresh. The animal's trail looped back and forth through the brush. This pattern told him the hare was loafing along, feeding here and there.

The fox lowered his nose to the ground and hurried after the hare. He made good time until he came to a granite outcropping. Here the thin layer of snow covering the rock had melted, erasing the hare's scent. The fox circled the bare patch. On the far side, he picked up the trail again.

The scent grew stronger — he was gaining ground. But to catch the hare, he must take it by surprise. If it saw him first, it would probably escape. The fox slowed his pace. Placing each foot with care, he moved as stealthily as a cat.

The trail led him into a grove of young spruce trees. Inside the grove the light was poor, and it was hard to see through the screen of evergreens. The fox stopped with one paw raised. His nose picked up a faint whiff of the hare's body scent. Slowly he turned his head to pinpoint the source.

•

The hare was crouched at the base of a spruce tree, nibbling the lower branches. While it chewed each mouthful of needles, it kept a sharp lookout for danger.

Once, the hare thought it saw a flash of color among the trees. Its ears went up, and it stood on its hind legs to get a better look. Everything appeared to be normal. After a minute or two, the hare resumed its meal.

The next time the hare turned round, it found itself looking into the yellow eyes of a fox. The fox was ready to spring. When the fox leapt at the hare, it jumped aside and bolted through the trees.

At first, the hare ran in a straight line. Then, when the fox had nearly caught up, the hare changed to a zigzag pattern. The fox couldn't follow the twists and turns, and tried to intercept the hare by cutting across its path. But the hare escaped each time by stopping suddenly and bounding off in a different direction.

Eventually the hare darted into a dense bramble thicket.

The fox gave up the chase.

From the safety of the thicket, the hare watched its pursuer lope across the field. On the far side of the field, the fox investigated a weedy ditch. He appeared to be searching for mice, and seemed to have forgotten the hare. Farther along, he slipped into the ditch. The last the hare saw of the fox was the white tip of his bushy tail disappearing through the weeds

•

The fox hadn't forgotten the hare, nor was he mousing — but he wanted the hare to think so. He knew that hares usually return to the place where the chase began. By pretending to hunt for mice, he hoped to trick the hare into dropping its guard.

At the end of the field, the fox followed another ditch that led back to the spruce grove. When he reached the grove, he discovered several well-worn paths used by hares. The fox cast around until he found one that passed close to the spot where the hare had been feeding. Then he lay down behind a tree to wait.

Soon he heard the soft thump of approaching feet. When the hare drew abreast, the fox sprang from his hiding place and seized it by the neck. The hare died instantly. Although he was hungry, the fox didn't eat his prey. Instead he picked it up and set off for the den. The meal was for his mate, the vixen.

•

He had met the vixen during a snowstorm in December. Both foxes had sought shelter under the same rock ledge. After the storm, they hunted as a pair. In February they became mates. In March, the vixen had prepared a birthing den. When the fox left her the previous night, she was about to have her litter.

•

The fox threaded his way through the overgrown field until he came to an old split-rail fence. On the other side of the fence was an abandoned railroad. Easing under the fence, he jumped the ditch and climbed the embankment. Cautiously he looked both ways before stepping onto the graveled right-of-way.

By now the sun was directly overhead. Except for a few shaded areas, the last traces of the morning snow had melted, leaving a dun-colored landscape.

As the fox trotted along, his orange coat contrasted sharply with the drab background. At the end of a long bend, he caught sight of the den.

It had been dug into the gravel at the base of the embankment. Originally it had been a woodchuck's burrow. The vixen had taken care to choose a well drained site. She knew that if water seeped into the birthing chamber, her babies could perish. Before moving into the den, she had given it a thorough housecleaning, and enlarged the main tunnel. The entrance — which she also enlarged — faced south to take advantage of the sun.

•

The fox looked over his shoulder to make sure that he hadn't been followed, before descending the slope. At the entrance to the den, he paused again to check for danger. Inside he could hear tiny whimpers and squeaks. Carrying the hare in his mouth, he padded along the tunnel to join his mate. But the vixen, concerned for the safety of her newborn kits, growled at him to stay out of the chamber. The fox dropped the hare at the entrance, and left. On a rise of ground nearby — where he could keep an eye on the den — he lay down to rest.

The vixen had given birth to five kits. Like all red foxes, they were born blind and deaf. As each one came into the world, she groomed it with her tongue then fed it with her milk.

The kits were about the size of chipmunks, with blunt heads and stubby noses. Except for the pink soles of their feet, they were covered with soft gray fur. The only similarity to their parents was the white tips of their tails.

Four of the five babies were males. The first to be born and the largest of the males was Sandy. His brothers were Rusty, Snap, and Swifty. The last to be born, and the smallest in the litter, was a female. Her name was Amber.

CHAPTER TWO

THE INTRUDER

It was the last Saturday in April. Along the right-of-way, clumps of coltsfoot bloomed like yellow dandelions. On the sunny slopes white strawberry flowers showed through the faded grass. At the base of the embankment, the pussy willow catkins were covered in silver fur. Near the den a Song sparrow sang, *Sweet, sweet, sweet,* followed by musical trills and whistles.

•

Amber and her brothers slept, snuggled against their mother. The vixen had stayed with the litter since their birth. Without her constant attention and the warmth of her fur, the little ones wouldn't have survived the cold.

Amber's eyes opened when she was ten days old.
Her eyes were blue. As she grew older, they would
change to a golden color. The centers of her eyes —
the pupils — weren't round like a dog, but upright
slits like a cat. Nature gave foxes vertical pupils to
help them see in bright sunlight as well as at night.

The kits had doubled their weight in their first
two weeks. Despite their rapid growth, they were
barely able to crawl. And, though their eyes had
opened, they still used their sense of smell to locate a
meal. Even so, they often grabbed a mouthful of their
mother's stomach fur by mistake. When this
happened, they kept nosing around until they found
a nipple. Between feedings they slept.

•

Amber's father was at his observation post on the hill.
From where he lay, he could watch the den and the
surrounding countryside. The breeze brought him the
scent of fresh-turned earth from the fields on the far
side of the rail line. In the distance, he could hear the
faint hum of a tractor.

The sun felt good on his silky coat but made him
sleepy. As the morning went on, he had to struggle to
keep awake. Once again he scanned the area on both

sides of the den. Everything seemed fine — until his gaze reached the far end of the rail line. He sat up to get a better look.

Near the farm two humans and a dog had appeared on the right-of-way. They were some distance off, but they were coming toward him.

•

After the boys finished their chores, they wondered what to do for the rest of the morning. One of them suggested a hike along the abandoned rail line. It was just a few minutes walk from the barn, at the bottom of the cornfield.

The older boy used a wooden fence post for support when he climbed the fence. His younger brother, who was only seven, tried to climb the wire between the posts, and had to be helped over. The dog had no difficulty. It quickly found a low spot and squeezed under the fence. Then the three of them climbed the embankment and set off down the right-of-way.

Although it was too early for the leaves to be out, the fields were dotted with spring birds. Glossy black grackles, meadowlarks, and bright-breasted robins were among the new arrivals. In the marshy places, red-winged blackbirds swayed on cattails, singing, *Konk-a-lee, konk-a-lee, konk-a-lee!*

The boys had been walking for about ten minutes when another sound, like faintly squeaking wheels, drifted from the sky. Both boys looked up.

The younger one pointed with his stick. "There they are!" he cried.

Silhouetted against the clouds, a ragged vee of Canada geese was beating its way north. As the flock passed overhead, they could hear the voice of the leader, *Ahonk, ahonk, ahonk!*

•

The boys began to drag their feet as they neared the old bridge. The bridge was as far as they were allowed to go. After the railroad was abandoned, the rails had been taken up and the bridge had been dismantled. Now all that was left were two rusty beams over the stream. The boys had been told by their parents it was too dangerous to cross.

Bounding ahead, the dog disappeared down the slope. Moments later they saw him at the edge of the stream. Fed by melting snow, the stream had overflowed its banks. The dog ran along the bank, casting about for a place to cross, then plunged into the rushing water.

The boys held their breaths as they watched the big dog splash his way to the other side. Once ashore, the dog shook himself and continued on with his nose to the ground. He was following something. The trail took him along the ditch then veered toward the railroad bed.

Wagging his tail with excitement, the dog sniffed around the hole in the embankment. By the time the boys called him, his head was in the hole and gravel was flying in all directions.

The older boy shook his head "He won't listen." Squinting at the sun, he added, "It must be about noon, we'd better start back or we'll be late for lunch."

"What about the dog?" asked his brother.

"He knows his way home."

•

The vixen pricked up her ears at the dog's approach. She couldn't see anything from her chamber, but she could hear the dog sniffing at the entrance to the tunnel. After a brief silence, she heard it clawing at the gravel.

She knew she could escape through the hidden opening or "bolt hole" off the main tunnel. But this

would mean deserting her kits. Although she was frightened, she wouldn't leave her litter.

As the sounds of digging grew louder, the vixen's heart beat faster and she began to pant. Drawing her kits close, she growled in her throat and bared her teeth. If the intruder forced his way in, she would defend her babies with her life

•

The vixen's mate watched anxiously from his hiding place on the hill. He had hoped the dog wouldn't cross the swollen stream. Now it was digging furiously at the entrance to his den. The dog was too big to attack. There was only one thing the fox could do. He would have to lure the dog away.

The fox trotted boldly down the slope. Opposite the den, he stopped in a little clearing. When the dog paused to shake the gravel from his coat, the fox gave two high-pitched barks. The dog backed out of the hole and looked around. The fox yapped again to catch his attention. For a moment the dog was so surprised to see the fox that he didn't move. Then with a deep-throated *Woof!*, he charged the fox.

The fox jumped aside and ran up the hill with the dog snapping at his heels. At the top of the hill the fox headed for the forest. Gradually the fox lengthened his lead but made sure the dog could always see him. He didn't want his pursuer to lose heart.

The outcome of the chase was never in question. With his fine bones and powerful, long legs the fox could run all day. He also knew every nook and cranny of the surrounding countryside. The dog, though bigger and stronger, was much slower and didn't know the territory.

The fox led the dog in a big circle through the forest, then crossed the stream and headed back toward the farm. After twenty minutes, the fox could hear the dog gasping for breath as he pounded along behind him. At this point — having exhausted his enemy and led him far from the den — the fox decided to end the chase. With a flick of his bushy tail, he vanished into the undergrowth.

•

As soon as he was rid of the dog, the fox went straight back to the den. At the entrance he coughed twice to tell his mate he was coming in. Then he crawled along the tunnel to her chamber. The two foxes happily touched noses in greeting.

The vixen was relieved that her mate had survived the chase. But she was still deeply worried. An enemy had tried to break into the den, and she knew it was only a matter of time before the enemy would return.

While her pups slept and her mate kept watch, the vixen listened uneasily for the intruder's return. In March, when she had prepared the den in the embankment, she had also cleaned out another den. The second den was some distance from the rail line and was to be used in an emergency.

As soon as it was dark, she would move her babies to the other den.

CHAPTER THREE

THE ELM TREE DEN

The vixen emerged from the den just after sunset. By then, the color had left the sky and the countryside had darkened to shades of gray. It was the twilight hour, when night creatures begin their rounds and owls take wing.

Sitting quietly by the entrance, the mother fox looked and listened. From every side came the fluting peeps of frogs. In the field, a robin sang goodbye to the day, *Cheer-up, cheer-up, cheer-up!* Over the evening chorus, she heard her mate call softly from the hill.

At the sound of his bark, the vixen turned and went back into the den. Two minutes later, she reappeared with one of her kits in her mouth. It was Sandy, the biggest male. She paused to check for danger, then started up the slope.

When the vixen reached the top of the hill, her mate came out of the shadows to join her. They walked together for a short distance, then parted in different directions. That night he would hunt while she moved the kits to their new home.

•

The vixen trotted across the pasture to the rail fence, then followed the fence until she reached the old elm tree. The entrance to the new den was half-hidden among the roots of the tree. It had been dug by a woodchuck, used briefly by a skunk, and later enlarged by a family of raccoons. When the mother fox took over the den, she had only cleaned out the nearest chamber. Farther along the tunnel there were more rooms and several bolt holes.

Before entering the new den, the vixen looked behind to make sure she hadn't been followed. Then she slipped down the passage with her baby. After leaving Sandy, she hurried back to fetch another kit. She had to be quick because Sandy would soon get chilled, lying alone on the cold earth floor.

Amber was the next to be carried to the new den. At the touch of her mother's teeth on her neck, she

gave a squeak of fright and curled into a ball. The
journey passed in a blur. She heard Sandy
whimpering when she was dropped beside him. The
two kits crawled together for warmth. At that
moment they formed a bond.

In the next hour they were joined by Rusty, Snap,
and Swifty. With each new arrival, the whining of the
hungry kits grew louder. But their mother couldn't
stop to suckle them until the last one had been
transferred. Then she fed them all. Just before dawn
their father — who had followed the vixen's trail to
the new den — brought a muskrat to feed their
mother. By first light the family was asleep, safe in
their new home.

•

The young foxes grew quickly. At the beginning of
May, when they were three weeks old, they took their
first shaky steps. They kept bumping into each other
in the cramped space but soon learned to control their
feet. Within a few days they were scampering around
the den. By this time they had also grown milk teeth,
including two sets of pointed fangs. Now that they
could move about freely, and they had teeth, their
behavior changed. They began to roughhouse.

Without warning one would attack the other. Sometimes three or four would get into a brawl, biting whoever was in range of their needle-sharp teeth. Even when a kit squeaked with pain, the vixen didn't try to stop them. For foxes of this age, their behavior was normal. They fought to establish their place in the litter. Sandy, being the strongest, was the winner. Rusty was next in line. Amber didn't enjoy fighting, but she was quick on her feet and able to hold her own with Snap and Swifty. She and her two brothers competed with each other at the bottom of the pecking order.

The pecking order was mainly about food. Food wasn't a problem while their mother was nursing them, as she could feed them all at the same time. Once weaned, a kit's position in the pecking order could mean the difference between a full stomach and an empty one.

•

By the time they were four weeks old, the kits' faces had become more pointed and their legs had lengthened. Their coats had also changed from charcoal gray to brownish gray, and the fur on their white-tipped tails was longer. At this age their mother began to leave them for short periods. She never went far, and she always returned in time to feed them.

One morning, while their mother was away, the kits explored the tunnel. Drawn by the scent of fresh air, they crept along the narrow tunnel to the entrance. Sandy was the first to peek outside. Amber and her brothers, overcome by curiosity, soon joined him. Squashed together in the entrance hole, the five little foxes blinked in the bright sunlight and looked around in wonder. The outside world was so different from their dark chamber. And there was so much to see!

While they were absorbed in the view, a gust of wind swept a dead leaf from the grass. The leaf flipped up in the air, then glided back to earth. On its short journey, it passed over the entrance hole. The sight of the leaf bearing down on them terrified the kits. Tumbling over each other in their haste to escape, they fled back down the tunnel.

After this fright they stayed in their chamber. A few days later the vixen called the kits outside. Because of their encounter with the leaf, it took half an hour of coaxing for them to join her. On their first outing none of the babies left her side.

Soon, however, they recovered their confidence. The next day, when the vixen called them, the kits came out of the den with a rush. No longer timid, they played happily with their mother. She let them climb all over her and even let them pounce on her swishing tail. Now it was time for their first lesson. They must learn the danger signal.

The vixen walked a short distance from the entrance and barked twice. Amber and the others looked up for a moment then went back to their play. She barked again. None of the kits paid any attention. Suddenly the vixen dashed at the surprised youngsters. Repeating the same bark, she rounded them up and chased them into the den.

The lesson was tested the following afternoon. Amber and her brothers were playing outside when their father noticed a speck circling in the sky. It was a red-tailed hawk. At their father's bark, the youngsters bolted into the den. Their father remained outside and watched the hawk until it sailed out of sight.

When the kits were five weeks old, their mother began to wean them from milk to solid food. Her first step was to leave a dead mouse outside the entrance to the den. Sandy came upon the mouse and sniffed it. Then he took a bite. He didn't try to eat the mouse but only sucked its juices. Amber saw him lick his chops, and went over. Sandy allowed her to take a bite. The taste was different from her mother's milk, but she liked it.

After all the kits had begun to eat meat, their mother suckled them less often. When she didn't want to nurse, she would lie on her belly and push a mole or a vole toward them. At first her little ones cried and wouldn't touch these offerings. They even tried to suckle their father, but when they nosed at his stomach fur, he jumped aside. Eventually the kits became so hungry between nursings that they were forced to eat solid food. Slowly they grew to like red meat.

While they were being weaned, Amber and her brothers continued to sleep in the den. If both parents went hunting, they were left alone. Whenever the kits left the den, one parent was always there to keep an eye on them.

As the days passed, the kits spent more time above ground. There was lots of room to play outside. They played until they fell asleep from exhaustion —

sometimes in the middle of a game. Hide-and-go-seek, chase, and follow-the-leader were among the most popular games.

Their favorite game, which they played endlessly, was stalking. The object of this game was to creep up on your victim and catch him by surprise. It was especially rewarding if you could pounce on him while he was sleeping or studying a bug in the grass.

The stalking game taught Amber to walk softly and to pounce with precision. She also learned to keep an ear cocked for danger, even when she was sleeping.

There was much more to these games than Amber realized. They were Nature's way of developing and sharpening her survival skills. She was being prepared for the time — now only a few months away — when she would be on her own.

CHAPTER FOUR

SUMMER

The first rays of dawn swept the pasture, lighting the dewdrops that clung to the grass. In a few hours the purple violets at the base of the elm tree and the buttercups along the fence line would open their petals to the sun. It was going to be a fine June day.

Amber and her brothers stirred restlessly in the den. They were hungry. During the past few weeks their feeding schedule had been gradually changed. Now they were only fed in the early morning and the evening.

At the sound of their father's muffled bark, they rushed out to meet him. He had caught a red squirrel and a field mouse. Sandy, the boss of the litter, was the first to approach his parent. Wagging his tail and whining, Sandy crept forward and licked the corners of his father's mouth. His father let him have the squirrel.

While Sandy fought off Snap and Swifty, who were trying to steal his meal, Amber begged the dead mouse from her father. But before she reached the den, Snap and Swifty saw what had happened and chased after her. One of them nipped her on the shoulder and she dropped the mouse.

Both of her brothers grabbed it, and neither would let go. The two young foxes dug their hind feet into the ground and began a tug-of-war. Growling fiercely, they jerked their heads this way and that. The contest ended when the mouse tore in two.

Amber had already turned away and was hunting for her breakfast. The first thing she found was a large June bug that had crashed into the grass during the night. Pinning the bug with her paw, she bent down and popped it into her mouth. Nearby, she found another June bug. Then she saw a spotted frog. It took three pounces to catch the frog, but it was worth the effort. The rest of her meal consisted of wild strawberries, a fruit that foxes love.

Amber was used to going hungry. Her parents gave out food on a first-come first-served basis. Being the smallest in the litter, she was often pushed aside. To survive, she had to rely on her wits. At dusk and dawn she would wait by the entrance to be the first in line. Even if she managed to get some food, this only solved part of her problem. Her next challenge was to keep the meal long enough to eat it.

Amber had discovered an unused room farther back in the tunnel. It was small and it had a musty odor from its former occupant, a skunk. None of her brothers knew about this chamber. It was a place where she could eat in peace — her secret hideout.

She also kept some of her toys — a pebble, a stick, the leg bone of a hare, and a bird's wing — in the hideout. Opposite the chamber, there was a bolt hole that led from the tunnel to the ground above. Amber sometimes used the bolt hole to listen for her parents' return.

•

The kits were weaned in early June, when they were eight weeks old. By now they were more than half grown. They were beginning to look like adult foxes, with tawny fur on their sides and back, white underparts, black stockings, and sausage-shaped tails. The color of their eyes had also changed from blue to gold.

Their parents looked ragged and worn. The adults were in the middle of their annual molt, and their long winter fur was falling out in tufts. The sun had bleached the remaining fur a dirty yellow. To add to the patchwork appearance of their coats, the new fur growing in was shorter than the old.

•

On the other side of the forest, a pair of bald eagles had a nest by the lake. The nest was a huge mass of sticks wedged into the fork of a tall beech tree. In the nest were two baby eagles covered with gray down. The eaglets were growing quickly and needed more food each day. On this June morning, it was the mother eagle's turn to hunt while her mate kept watch over the nest.

After circling the nest, the mother eagle soared over the lake. She was looking for dead fish floating on the surface. Her search turned up nothing. She then glided over the beach, hoping to find a fish that had been washed ashore. When this too proved fruitless, she flew inland.

The trees in the forest were so close together that she couldn't see the ground below. When she reached the far side of the forest, she landed in a tree. In the distance was the rail line, below her were the fields. Perched on a dead limb, the eagle surveyed the pasture with fierce yellow eyes.

•

That morning Sandy, Rusty, and Snap went hunting with their father. After they left, the vixen took a nap under a juniper bush. Amber and Swifty, (who hadn't had any food), went in search of their breakfast. The two soon found a patch of strawberries a little way from the den.

Neither of the young foxes noticed the great, dark bird in the tree. They were concentrating on the ground, gobbling berries as fast as they could find them. They fed side by side until the patch began to thin. Then Amber looked around and spied another clump of strawberries.

•

The eagle saw the young foxes as soon as she landed in the pine. The kits were in the open, and neither parent was in sight. The eagle was certain she would get one of them. The only question in her mind was which of the two she would take. She chose the nearest one — Amber.

Just as the eagle launched herself from the branch, Amber stepped behind a bush. The eagle, coming in fast and low, swung to the side and went for the other kit. At the instant of contact, her sharp claws closed on Swifty, piercing his heart. The huge bird pulled out of her dive with the kit in her talons, and rose smoothly into the air.

Amber didn't know what had happened. She was bending to pick a berry when she heard the rush of wings. Instinctively she flattened herself against the ground. By the time she turned around, Swifty was gone and the eagle was climbing into the sky.

Alerted by Swifty's cry, the vixen raced to the strawberry patch, but it was too late. The eagle had already cleared the trees and was heading back to the lake. There was nothing she could do.

•

That evening the kits played outside the den, as usual. At twilight, they heard an owl call softly from the woods, *Hoo, hoo-hoo-hoo, hoo, hoo*. The vixen and her mate pricked up their ears. After a short silence, the low notes were repeated, *Hoo, hoo-hoo-hoo, hoo, hoo*.

It was the call of a great horned owl, the most ferocious owl in the forest.

The adult foxes weren't afraid for themselves, but they knew this owl could take one of their kits. The next time the owl hooted, the sound seemed closer. The vixen, having just lost one of her young, was taking no chances. She barked twice and sent the kits into the den.

Later that night, when her parents returned from hunting, Amber was given a red-backed vole. The vole looked like a plump mouse with a chestnut stripe on its back. Amber preferred voles to mice as they had more meat on their bones. Now that she had her permanent teeth, she no longer had to pick voles to pieces but could chew them whole.

The following evening, the vixen took Amber and Sandy for a hunting lesson. She led the way, and the kits followed in single file. When they started off, both Amber and Sandy kept straying from the path, but a few nips from their mother settled them down. She wanted their full attention.

Presently the vixen caught a mouse. Rather than crushing it, she carried it gently to an open spot in the pasture. Then she dropped the mouse between

Amber and Sandy. The mouse righted itself and started to run. Sandy made a pounce, but missed, and the mouse scurried toward Amber.

As it went past, Amber shot out a black paw and neatly trapped the little animal. After a moment she lifted her paw to see if it was still there. This was a mistake. While she was checking, the mouse used the few seconds to make its escape.

Amber still had a lot to learn.

CHAPTER FIVE

LESSONS

The hum of cicadas marked the close of another hot July day. The hayfield beside the pasture was awash with daisies, buttercups, and Queen Anne's lace. Amber, half-hidden in the long grass, was stalking a monarch butterfly. But each time she got close to her prey, it danced out of range. At last the orange and black butterfly settled on a tall milkweed plant.

The young vixen was about to leap when she heard a rustle in the grass. Whirling around, she saw that Sandy had crept up behind her. Instantly forgetting the butterfly, she dashed away with her brother in pursuit. The two foxes raced about the field, leaving a cloud of dandelion seeds in their wake.

Both were panting by the end of their romp.

Amber shook the seeds from her coat and licked a flower petal off her nose. Then she sat down and combed out the remaining seeds with her teeth. When this was done, she stretched out on her stomach to cool off.

A few minutes later, she looked across at Sandy and wagged her tail, inviting him to play again. Growling fiercely, the two got into a shoving match, then tore off through the field in another game of chase.

•

Although the kits still spent a lot of time in play, their daily routine had changed in a number of ways. Since the beginning of July they had been sleeping outside the den. When they got hungry between feedings, they had to forage for themselves. In late summer this wasn't a problem as there was plenty to eat nearby, including grasshoppers, raspberries, and blueberries.

Serious lessons began when the kits were three months old. From then on they went hunting with their parents most nights. By watching the adults, they learned how to stalk and catch a variety of small animals. After being shown how it was done, the kits were left to make kills on their own. At first Amber and her brothers found it difficult, and their prey usually escaped. After a few weeks of practice, however, they became quite good at catching mice and voles. This was a vital skill for the young foxes' survival, as mice and voles were staples of their diet. By the end of the summer the kits were able to track — and sometimes catch — hares, muskrats, and woodchucks.

On these outings the kits also learned to avoid certain woodland animals. One evening Amber chanced upon a young skunk separated from its family. She was all set to play with the little black and white stranger, when the skunk's mother appeared. The mother skunk had raised her tail and was about to spray Amber when the vixen barked a warning.

Another time, when she was hunting with her father, Amber picked up the scent of a porcupine. Following her nose, she nearly bumped into the slow-moving animal. The porcupine raised its quills and lashed its tail at her. Unaware of the danger, she moved a step closer. At that moment her father rushed out of the shadows and bowled her over. If he hadn't knocked her away, Amber would certainly have got a face full of barbed quills, and might have died.

At the end of the nightly lessons the kits were
often left by their parents to find their own way
home. Their parents also encouraged them to hunt
for themselves by lengthening the time between
feedings and leaving food farther away from the den.

•

One hot afternoon the sky grew dark and lightning
flashed across the horizon. Moments later there was a
rumble of thunder. At the first few drops of rain, the
whole fox family took shelter in the den. Soon rain
was drumming on the hard-packed earth above them,
and water was trickling down the tunnel.

The storm led to an unusual lesson for the kits.
After the sky cleared, the family went worm hunting
in the pasture. The downpour had flooded the worms
out of their underground homes, and they were lying
in full view on the surface.

Worms were everywhere. All Amber had to do was
to choose the biggest one and pick it up. As the
ground began to dry, however, the worms began to
crawl back down their holes. Now she had to move
quickly to catch them. Catching the worms was only
part of the challenge.

Amber caught a fat worm that was halfway down

its hole. When she tried to pull it out of the ground, the worm stretched but wouldn't budge. Holding her end of the worm tightly, she gave it a jerk. The worm broke in two. The same thing happened with the next worm.

After several failures, Amber went over to her mother to see how it was done. The vixen caught the worm gently in her front teeth and, using her tongue as a guide, slowly lifted her head to ease the worm out of the hole. When the worm pulled free, she sucked it into her mouth like a piece of spaghetti.

•

One morning in August, a tractor with a hay mower lumbered into the field beside the pasture. For the rest of the day the mower clanked and banged around the hayfield. By late afternoon the field had been transformed from a sea of tall grass to bare stubble.

When the humans left, the mother fox took her kits to the field. She was going to give them another lesson. The whirring blades of the mower had not only cut the hay, but had also destroyed birds' nests and countless mice and voles.

The foxes picked their way through the stubble, feasting on the victims of the mower. When they

could eat no more, the vixen showed them a skill that
could save their lives in the future — how to store
food. Picking up a dead mouse, she carried it to the
edge of the field.

Curious to see what she was going to do, the kits
followed her. The vixen laid the mouse on the ground
and dug a shallow hole with her paws, keeping the
earth in a neat pile. Then, to their surprise, she
dropped the mouse into the hole. With her nose, she
carefully pushed the earth over the mouse until it was
completely hidden.

Copying their mother, each of the kits buried a
mouse. Amber's first attempt was a failure. Instead of
keeping the earth in a neat pile so that she would
have the loose soil to fill in the hole, she spread it
carelessly about. As a result, she had to move her
mouse and dig another hole.

The following day the vixen returned to the field
with her kits to see if they could find their mice.
They remembered roughly where they had buried
them, but it took a lot of sniffing to locate the exact
spot. Amber found her mouse first. Then a brief
scuffle broke out when Rusty dug up Sandy's mouse.
Snap made the mistake of burying his so deeply that

he couldn't smell it, nor could anyone else. It was never found.

Like most foxes, the vixen disliked snakes. When they were leaving the field that day, she noticed a garter snake. In a flash she pounced on the harmless snake and bit it behind the head. Then she threw it aside and continued on. The kits couldn't resist giving the snake a nervous sniff as they passed by. It had a musty odor.

One day Amber caught what she thought was a frog. But, unlike the smooth green frogs she'd eaten before, this one had a pebbly brown skin. It wasn't a frog — it was a toad. When she took her first bite, the oil in the toad's skin seeped into her mouth. It tasted terrible! It was so bad that she had to lick the ground to get rid of the taste. From then on, she never mistook a toad for a frog.

•

By mid-September, summer was drawing to a close. Song birds were gathering in flocks, and some had already left for the south. Mushrooms sprouted in the pasture overnight, and at dawn there were cobwebs on the dew-soaked grass. Goldenrod and purple asters bloomed along the borders of the field. Below the rail line, the swamp maples had begun to turn scarlet.

The kits were now almost full grown, with long pumpkin-colored coats. During the past month they had seen less and less of their parents. Gradually the family ties were loosening. Often the kits would go hunting by themselves or in pairs. Amber and Sandy usually hunted together. Sometimes the two were gone for several days.

The fox family split up in the last week of September. Sandy was the first to strike out on his own. One morning Amber woke to find that her partner had gone. Rusty and Snap went their separate ways a few days later. Amber also felt restless but stayed around the den waiting in vain for Sandy to return.

She saw her mother for the last time at the beginning of October. The vixen was friendly but gave no sign that she wanted her daughter to join her. The family bonds had broken. That evening Amber decided it was time to leave.

She had no idea where she would go.

CHAPTER SIX

AUTUMN

Amber left home that night under the orange glow of a harvest moon. When she reached the slope overlooking the abandoned rail line, she stopped to consider her next move. She decided to follow the right-of-way, a path she had traveled many times. Mounting the gravel embankment, she set off in the direction of the farm.

On the way she passed the den where she had been born six months ago. Farther along she came to the break in the right-of-way and the remains of the bridge across the stream. Ignoring the long drop to the water below, she stepped confidently onto one of the beams. Then, using her tail like a tightrope walker to keep her balance, she walked to the other side.

The last time she'd crossed the stream, she'd been

with Sandy, and they'd raced each other to the far
side. Now Sandy had gone and she was on her own.
Because she was alone, she knew she must take extra
care. Instead of trotting down the middle of the gravel
right-of-way, she walked slowly and stayed close to the
bordering foliage.

A sudden rustling in the leaves gave her a fright.
Had she been hunting with Sandy, she might have
whirled and pounced at the sound. Tonight safety was
her first concern.

High overhead she heard the clamor of geese.
Amber listened with her head cocked toward the sky.
As the birds drew closer, her sensitive ears picked out
the cries of different flocks. Then she saw a wavering
line of Canada geese silhouetted against the full
moon. They were flying south.

After the geese passed, she looked behind and in
front of her. Ahead, she noticed something move at
the base of a poplar tree. Amber stood on her hind
legs to get a better look.

Even then, she couldn't see what was making the
disturbance. Keeping low, she tip-toed forward. As
she drew closer, she heard the crackle of dry leaves,
and realized that the animal was about to emerge

from the undergrowth. Tensely, she waited for it to
appear.

A large black porcupine shambled out onto the
gravel. It had been feeding in the poplar tree and still
had a half-chewed yellow leaf in its mouth. Amber
knew that, as long as she kept her distance, the
porcupine wouldn't attack her. Giving it a wide berth,
she continued on her journey.

When the farm buildings came into view, she
decided not to go any farther. The young vixen didn't
want to be seen by the farm dog, as she and her
brother had nearly been caught by him a few weeks
ago. She was also tired from the strain of traveling by
herself. The stars were still bright in the sky when she
left the path and bedded down in a thicket.

She slept lightly — opening an eye every few
minutes — for the rest of the night. At first light she
heard the crunch of hooves on the gravel roadbed.
Amber stepped out of the thicket to see who was
coming. It was a mother deer with her two fawns.
They were browsing the foliage along the edge of the
right-of-way.

Amber was hungry, but she didn't want to risk
hunting in the daylight. To avoid being seen, she

planned to hunt and travel under the cover of darkness. Taking care not to show herself, she managed to find a few mouthfuls of berries from a nearby hawthorn bush.

She was chewing the last of the red berries when she noticed a flicker of movement in a clump of weeds. The young vixen stared at the spot. A mouse clung to one of the weed stems, eating seeds. Very quietly she moved closer. The mouse, sensing danger, stopped eating and looked up. When it saw the fox, it leapt to the ground and dashed for safety.

Amber pounced on the mouse and pinned it between her paws. A quick bite of her sharp teeth killed it. Then she tossed the mouse's body into the air and deftly caught it in her mouth.

Crunching the bones, she ate the mouse — fur and all. It wasn't much of a meal, but it eased the pangs of hunger.

Around mid-morning, she heard a sharp whistle. She recognized the sound, and went to the edge of the embankment to see if she could spot the woodchuck. After a minute or two the woodchuck whistled again. It was sitting like a brown post by its den at the far end of the pasture.

Amber knew how she could catch it. But it would mean crossing the open pasture in broad daylight. Torn between the fear of showing herself and the emptiness of her stomach, she considered the problem. The prospect of a meal of fat woodchuck made up her mind.

She went down the embankment, crossed the ditch, and slipped under the single strand of electric wire into the pasture. One of the cows looked up, and soon the whole herd was staring at her. Ignoring the cattle, the fox trotted toward the woodchuck's den. The woodchuck also saw her and fled down its burrow.

The moment the woodchuck disappeared, she hurried forward. The entrance hole to the den was on a little rise of ground, rimmed with earth. Rather than approaching it from the front, she crept in from the side. She went as close to the hole as she dared, and lay down with the breeze in her face. Because she was downwind, the woodchuck wouldn't smell her. Now all she had to do was wait.

It wasn't long before she heard a scrabbling sound in the tunnel. Moments later, she saw the top of the woodchuck's head. Amber flattened her body behind the rim of earth. With only its nose showing, the woodchuck looked around. Then it glanced at the sky and sniffed the breeze. Finally it decided it was safe to come out.

The instant the woodchuck emerged, Amber grabbed it by the neck. Her long canine teeth quickly ended the struggle. She would have liked to have eaten it on the spot, but it was too dangerous to remain in the open. Picking up her prize, she started for the embankment.

She didn't know that a crow, sitting silently in a tree, had been watching her.

As soon as she started across the pasture, the crow left its perch and flew over her, *Caaaw! Caaaaw! Caaaaw!* At the sound of the call, a flock of crows lifted from a nearby cornfield. The flock swirled above the fox, *Caaaw! Caaaaaw! Caaaaaw!* Then the big black birds began diving at her.

There was no place to hide.

Amber broke into a run to escape the screaming mob. But she couldn't outrun her attackers. Nor could she avoid them by swerving from side to side. As the crows became more excited, they became bolder.

Amber knew that they wanted the woodchuck, but she was determined to hold onto it, even though it slowed her down. The embankment wasn't far away. If she could just reach the sheltering trees, she would be safe.

She winced when a crow's claws raked her ear, but kept on going. Another crow came tearing in and struck her, with its beak, below her eye. It hurt so much that she gave a yelp of pain — and dropped the woodchuck. When she tried to pick it up again, the crows swarmed in from all sides, buffeting her with their wings, beaks, and claws. Amber realized she was beaten, and fled.

•

Late that afternoon Amber watched the crows leave the fields and fly in straggling lines to their roost. Even though she'd seen them go, and she was weak with hunger, she waited until it was dark to return to the pasture. The crows had picked the woodchuck clean. All that remained were a few scraps of fur and some bones.

There was nothing else to eat in the pasture, so she continued on to the cornfield. The corn had recently been cut, and the harvesting machine had left a lot of broken husks in the stubble. Amber loved corn, but before eating, she checked for danger.

She wasn't the only one in the field. To her right, three young raccoons were feeding with their mother. To her left, a skunk was scooping kernels from the ground. On the other side of the field, a black bear and her cub were stuffing themselves in the moonlight.

To be on the safe side, Amber stayed close to the edge of the field. After the first mouthful of corn, she began to feel better. When she'd eaten as much as her stomach could hold, she returned to the right of way and bedded down in the thicket.

CHAPTER SEVEN

A WELCOME FRIEND

By mid-October the countryside was ablaze with color. Along the right-of-way yellow, orange, and red hardwood trees stood out like flames against the dark evergreens. As well as a time of bright colors, it was harvest time. Food was everywhere, from purple grapes and chokecherries to crimson rosehips, scarlet mountain ash berries, and the velvet fruit of the sumac.

At the base of the embankment, the milkweed pods had broken open to reveal rows of flat brown seeds with silky tails. The slightest puff of wind sent these seeds sailing away like tiny parachutes. The tall burdock plants that grew among the milkweeds didn't need the help of the wind as their seeds had little hooks that stuck to the fur of passing animals.

•

Amber lay in the sun, camouflaged against the
patchwork of fallen leaves, pulling burdock seeds
from her tail. Each time she found a bur, she raked it
out with her teeth and spat it to the side. The long
red guard hairs had now come through her summer
fur, and her coat was thick and glossy. To keep it
clean and shiny, she groomed it every day.

The young fox didn't know that the trapping
season had just begun. Nor could she know that her
beautiful coat was worth money to trappers. The next
few months would be the most dangerous period in
her life.

•

Amber had been around the farm for nearly a week.
As the time passed, she had become familiar with her
new surroundings and settled into a natural routine.
During the daylight hours, she rested in the
undergrowth along the right-of-way. After dark, she
explored and hunted for food.

Most evenings she began her rounds with a visit to
the apple orchard. The orchard was close to the
farmhouse, so she had to be careful of humans and
the dog. Despite these dangers it was a favorite

feeding place, as there were plenty of mice, and the ground beneath the trees was littered with apples.

Between the house and the orchard stood a low wooden shed. Amber made a point of checking the shed on her way to and from the orchard. Every time she passed, she could smell the chickens inside, and often she could hear them clucking softly to each other, *Puk, puk, puk, puk.*

The farmer's wife kept the chickens for their eggs. During the day the chickens ranged freely outside. At night they were shut in the henhouse. The farmer's two boys had the chore of letting the hens out in the morning and seeing that they were safely inside before dark.

Amber was amazed at the tameness of the chickens. Hidden in the undergrowth, she often watched them pecking about the yard. The hens were so tame, they didn't even look up at the approach of the tractor, and they had to be shooed off the road to let it pass. It would be easy to catch one of those plump birds. So easy, she could almost taste it.

There were, however, obstacles to consider. The main problem was that the chickens were only outside during the day. If she tried to snatch one in the daylight, she was almost certain to be seen by one of the humans. Her parents had taught her to fear humans, and to avoid them.

The big farm dog was another problem. When the chickens were out, the dog was usually nearby. So far she had managed to avoid the dog, but if she made a daylight raid, the dog would see her and attack.

The only safe way to catch a chicken was after dark. For this reason she kept checking the henhouse each night. Her opportunity finally came at the end of the week.

The youngest boy — the seven-year-old — had been in a hurry when he closed the henhouse door, and the latch hadn't caught properly. When the fox passed by just after dusk, she saw to her surprise that the door was open a crack. Melting into the shadows, she waited to see what would happen. Half an hour passed and no human appeared.

Amber crept over to the henhouse, opened the door with her nose, and slipped inside. It took her a moment to get used to the strong smell in the silent room. The hens were in their nests on a long shelf opposite the door. Jumping lightly onto the shelf, she seized the nearest hen by the neck.

The hen's squawk alerted the rooster. The rooster's loud *Cock-a-doodle-doo* woke the rest of the occupants. Within moments all the chickens were clucking and flapping their wings, and the air was filled with bits of straw and feathers. Amber, holding the chicken in her mouth, jumped to the floor and made for the door.

The door had closed, shut by a gust of wind. She tried to push it open, but it wouldn't budge. Frantically, she looked around for another exit. There was no other way out.

She was trapped.

•

The farmer was on his way to the barn when he heard the uproar in the henhouse. From the commotion, he knew that some varmint — a weasel, a raccoon, or a fox — was attacking his chickens. He ran to get his gun. When he returned, his dog was already at the henhouse door, scratching to get in.

•

Amber was nervously pacing back and forth when the door suddenly opened. A blinding white light shone in her eyes. Stunned by the light, she dropped the chicken. At the same moment the dog lunged at her

and knocked her down. The two animals rolled around the floor, snarling and slashing at each other, while the flashlight beam darted after them.

The vixen's speed and agility had kept her from being seriously bitten, but she knew that if the fight continued, she would be killed. Jumping back, she feinted one way then changed direction and bolted for the door. She was so quick that the farmer, who was standing in the doorway, didn't realize what had happened. Before he could pin her in the beam of his flashlight, she had slipped between his legs and out the door.

The dog followed so closely that the farmer didn't dare shoot at the fox for fear of hitting his dog. As soon as she was outside, Amber made for the rail line. By the time she stopped for breath, the dog had given up the chase. Having made her escape, she trotted the rest of the way.

The events of the night meant that it was no longer safe for her to stay near the farm. She must move on. Rather than traveling through the fields, she decided to follow the rail line. The rail bed had a smooth gravel surface, and if she encountered danger, she could hide in the undergrowth a few steps away.

She traveled at a steady trot. Soon the familiar
landscape was behind her and she had entered
unknown territory. Before dawn she left the right-of-
way and bedded down in the undergrowth. Carefully
she chose a spot where she could see both the
embankment and the fields below it. Lying down
eased the hunger pains in her stomach. Even so, she
only slept for a few minutes at a time, and she
continually looked around to check for danger.

The sun had just cleared the horizon when she
saw something that brought her wide awake. It was a
fox! The fox was in the field below, following a fence
line. It was coming toward her. She could tell by its
shape and the way it moved that it was a male. But
with the low sun in her eyes, she couldn't make out
his coloring.

For a moment she thought he might be Sandy or
Rusty. Or her father. When the fox started up the
embankment, she saw his bright orange coat. It was
then that she realized he wasn't one of her family.

Amber stepped from her lair onto the right-of-
way. The stranger saw the young vixen and stopped.
Then the two foxes sat down and studied one
another. A minute or so later, they warily approached

each other. After some tense circling and sniffing, they finally touched noses.

Then Amber put her head between her paws and invited her new friend to play. The two foxes cavorted up and down the gravel path. It was the first time she had played since leaving home.

Her new friend's name was Flame. He was the same age as Amber, and he too had left his family.

The young foxes were delighted to meet, as both had been lonely. They stayed hidden in the undergrowth until sunset.

That night they hunted together.

CHAPTER EIGHT

DANGEROUS DAYS

Amber and Flame hunted most of the night and rested in the undergrowth the following day. Late that afternoon they were jerked awake by the sound of a gunshot. Both foxes jumped to their feet, ears cocked toward the marsh. A few minutes later they heard two more shots from the same direction, *Boom, boom!*

Amber had never heard a gun, and the noise of the explosions made her nervous. Flame was startled by the first blast, but when the shooting continued to come from the marsh, he relaxed. He had heard the humans in the marsh before.

The hunters left the marsh at dark. That night the foxes waited until the moon was up before setting out on their hunt. Flame led the way. When they emerged from some alders, Amber saw to her surprise that her new friend had taken her to the marsh.

The marsh occupied the shallow end of a lake. At first glance it looked like a giant hayfield. Patches of bulrushes, wild rice, and tall reeds were scattered here and there. When the young vixen stepped to the water's edge, she noticed that muskrats had cut narrow channels through the frost-faded grass, and there were many islands offshore.

The two foxes hunted the shoreline of the marsh. With noses close to the ground, they sniffed at the muskrat trails, the duck feathers that had been blown ashore, and even the empty clamshells that had been opened by raccoons. Once, they spotted a fat muskrat feeding on the bank. They tried to stalk the furry brown animal, but it saw them and quickly escaped into the water.

Farther along, they came upon the scent of a wounded duck. The duck had been shot by the hunters, and had swum ashore with a broken wing. Flame found the bird hiding in some weeds, and killed it. After tearing some feathers away, he and Amber ate the breast meat. Had the fox not caught the crippled bird, it would have died a slow death from starvation.

Rather than return to the rail line, Amber and Flame bedded down in the alders. The day was warm and sunny, and they heard little shooting from the marsh. During the time they rested, a seagull, a crow, and several white-footed mice fed on the duck's carcass.

The two foxes went back to the marsh that night. A tour of the shoreline revealed signs of muskrat activity, but they didn't see a single muskrat. Nor did they see any ducks, except for some mallards sleeping on the water far from shore. The foxes did manage to catch a few mice in the alders, but not enough to fill their stomachs.

Still hungry, they decided to try the edge of the marsh once more. It was growing light in the east when Amber spied a pair of ducks swimming in the weeds. The ducks were within pouncing distance of the shore. Quietly withdrawing from the water's edge, the foxes split up and began their stalk.

•

Half an hour before dawn the two men loaded their gear into the small boat and launched it into the water. Paddling silently, they followed a muskrat canal though the marsh. When they reached the pond, they stowed their paddles. While the boat drifted, they dropped a dozen wooden duck decoys in the water. To make their flock of decoys look more natural, they carefully placed two of the decoys close to the shore.

After setting out their decoys, the men pushed their drab-colored boat into a stand of bulrushes until it was hidden. They were now ready to hunt. One of the men lit a cigarette while the other poured cups of coffee from an insulated container. Pulling up the collars of their camouflage coats, they waited for the dawn.

Presently one of them said in a low voice, "It'll soon be light enough to shoot. Better load your gun."

Crouched in the boat with their guns at the ready, the hunters scanned the sky for ducks. One of them glanced at the pond to make sure the decoys were properly placed. Something caught his eye. He stared at it for a moment.

"Hey!" he hissed "There's a fox creeping up on our decoys!"

His companion peered through the reeds. "I see it," he whispered. "Look, there's another fox coming from the other side!"

"We'll fix those varmints!"

"O.K., but wait until they get closer," the second one replied. "I'll say when to shoot."

The men hunched forward, their faces hidden by the screen of rushes. It was difficult to see the approaching foxes as they kept low, their bellies close to the ground. When a fox passed behind a clump of weeds they would lose sight of it. Finally, both foxes were in the open.

"You shoot the one on the left and I'll take the one on the right," said the older hunter. A few seconds later, he added, "Now!"

The men slid their gun barrels through the rushes. One gun pointed at Amber, the other at Flame. As the hunters lined up their targets, the weight in the boat shifted slightly, dislodging a coffee cup. The metal cup landed with a loud clang on the bottom of the boat. The foxes jumped at the sound, and the guns roared at the same instant. Both foxes dropped from sight behind low weeds.

"We got 'em!"

Stowing their guns, the hunters picked up their paddles and pushed the boat out of the rushes. It took them less than two minutes to reach land. When they stepped ashore to pick up their trophies, they found nothing. The men walked back and forth, studying the ground. But there was not even a drop of blood.

The foxes had vanished.

•

In fact, neither fox had been hit. The falling coffee cup saved their lives. A split second before the hunters fired, the foxes had jumped at the sound — and the hunters had missed. But the pellets had come so close that the shock waves had bowled them over. For a few moments Amber and Flame lay stunned on the ground. Then, while the men's backs were turned as they pushed their boat from the rushes, the foxes recovered their feet and fled.

•

Amber ran blindly, her only thought to get away from the marsh. It wasn't until she came to a stream, that she stopped to catch her breath. After a brief rest and a drink, she looked around to get her bearings. Nothing looked familiar. To get a better view, she climbed a nearby ridge. In the distance, she saw a raised line of trees — the old railway.

She wondered about Flame. When the guns

roared, they had run in opposite directions. Perhaps
her friend had gone back to the railroad where they'd
first met. After dark she would try to find him. If he
wasn't on the right-of-way, she would hide in the
undergrowth and wait for him.

•

A brisk north wind was blowing across the right-of-
way when Amber climbed the embankment. The
wind made her nervous, because the rustle of the
leaves masked the sounds of the night. And the high
wind not only made it difficult to hear but it also
blew the scent away.

The young vixen stayed close to the edge of the
roadbed, on the alert for danger. In the distance she
saw an animal loping toward her. For a moment she
thought it was Flame. When four more animals
appeared behind the first one, she realized her
mistake.

They were wolves!

She had no time to lose. Instinctively choosing the
downwind side, she left the embankment and
followed a weed-filled ditch out into the fields. From
her hiding place, she watched as five gray shapes
loped silently past the spot where she had been

standing minutes before. The wolves didn't pick up her scent.

For now she was safe. But she didn't dare resume her journey, as they could easily return the same way they had come.

She worried that the wolves might have come upon Flame, and she wondered if she would ever see him again.

CHAPTER NINE

THE TRAP

By the end of October the cold north winds had stripped the maples of their brilliant colors. All that remained were a few brown or yellow leaves clinging to the oaks, birches, and poplars. From a distance the hardwood stands and the trees along the embankment looked smoky gray.

Since her encounter with the wolves, Amber had lived in the fields. During the daylight hours she stayed in the weed-filled ditches, and only left them after dark. She took these precautions because she knew the wolves were still in the area.

On the last night of October she heard a fox bark in the distance. The call was faint but sounded familiar. Amber quickly replied with two sharp barks.

After waiting for a few minutes without a response, she barked again.

She was about to go in search of the mysterious caller when she was stopped by a long, quavering howl, *Awooovv! awooooo!* From the sound, the wolf was somewhere between her and the other fox. Moments later she heard another drawn out call, *Awooooo! awooooo!* The second wolf was behind her!

Amber was terrified of wolves. She knew that she couldn't outrun a wolf. Nor could she stand and fight, as wolves hunted in packs and she was too small to face even a single wolf. By barking, she had revealed her position to the wolves. If she stayed where she was, the wolves would come upon her trail and hunt her down. Her only hope now was to outwit them.

Some years earlier a storm had toppled a dead elm tree, and the trunk lay in pieces at the base of the embankment. When she passed the spot a few days ago, the young vixen noticed that a skunk had made its winter home in one of the hollow lengths. This gave her an idea.

Leaving the field, she hurried to the dead tree. The section of trunk where the skunk lived had one end wedged against some boulders, and the other end in the grass. It was a tight squeeze, but she managed to enter the hollow trunk through the boulders. The skunk was curled in a ball, blocking the other end of the tunnel. When Amber appeared, the skunk studied her with beady black eyes, decided that the young fox wasn't a threat, and went back to sleep.

•

Within minutes one of the wolves had followed Amber's trail to the tree trunk. But the wolf was puzzled by the change in scent — from fox to skunk — and unsure what was in the hollow trunk. Cautiously he sniffed the surrounding grass and scratched at the opening with one paw. This disturbance was enough to wake the skunk, who turned around in the log and prepared to defend itself.

A second wolf, an old female, arrived on the scene. She had also followed Amber's trail and couldn't understand why the first wolf was so timid. Pushing the young wolf aside, the older wolf boldly thrust her snout into the opening. An instant later she received a blast of oily spray full in the face.

The wolf leapt from the hole with stinging eyes,

gagging at the taste. The young wolf also jumped back to avoid the smell — a stench so foul that it blocked out all other animal scents — including those left by a fox.

•

Amber was safe for the moment but feared the wolves would be back to look for her. She remembered a water-filled ditch that ran through the embankment to the fields on the other side of the rail line. With no attempt to hide her tracks, she trotted along the gravel right-of-way. When she reached the ditch, she descended the embankment to the overgrown field on the other side. The wolves, she knew, would pick up her scent on the right-of-way and follow it.

To mislead the wolves, she walked in circles around the weed field, then edged over to the flooded ditch and jumped into the water. Staying in the middle, she splashed down the ditch, through the culvert under the right-of-way, and out into the field on the other side. By walking in the water and taking care not to brush the weeds on the banks with her fur, she left no scent. After she was far out in the field, she left the flooded ditch and slipped into a small side ditch.

That night the temperature dropped below freezing. By dawn there was ice on the puddles, and the fields were white with frost.

Amber shifted her position in the weeds to catch the first rays of the morning sun. She had endured a long and stressful night. She'd managed to fool the wolves, however, and she knew they wouldn't return before nightfall. In the meantime she needed rest.

Around noon she was woken by the sound of a machine coming along the right-of-way. She looked around, but she couldn't see it from where she lay. To get a better view, she climbed out of the ditch and sat at the edge of the field. The machine was a small four-wheeled vehicle driven by a man. When the vehicle slowed to a stop opposite her, Amber leapt back into the ditch.

•

As he motored along, the man scanned the countryside. He could see the fields on both sides of the right-of-way through the bare trees. For a few seconds, his eye caught a splash of scarlet in one of the fields. He thought it might be a fox. The trapper stopped and got off his four-wheeler. By the time he had focused his binoculars, the fox had disappeared.

After he studied the spot through his glasses, the man noticed the line of the ditch. Now he knew where the fox had gone. He thought for a moment, then mounted his vehicle and continued along the right-of-way. As soon as he was out of sight around the next bend, he stopped again. From the cargo box behind his seat he pulled out a large canvas bag.

Slinging the bag over his shoulder, he clambered down the embankment and walked into the brush that bordered the rail line. When he came upon a pile of moss-covered rocks, he looked it over, then dropped the bag and knelt down. From the bag he withdrew an axe, a wooden stake, and a trap attached to a short length of steel cable.

In the narrow space between two large rocks he dug a shallow hole. Then he put a dead mouse in the hole and covered it lightly with earth — the same way a fox would bury a mouse. After placing the bait, he cleared a plate-sized patch in front of the opening for the trap.

Because the trap's coil springs were so strong, the man had to step on the side levers to cock the trap's steel jaws open. Carefully he laid the trap in the cleared patch so that it was level with the ground. To

secure the trap, he drove the stake into the ground
with the back of his axe and attached the steel cable.
The cable was then hidden with dead leaves, and the
trap was covered with a layer of damp earth. As a
finishing touch, the man sprinkled a handful of leaves
on top of the earth.

This arrangement, known as a "dirt hole set," was
one of the trapper's favorite ways to catch a fox. By
putting the bait between the rocks, he forced the fox
to approach it from only one direction. When the fox
moved forward to sniff the bait, it would step on the
hidden trap, and the jaws would snap shut on its
foot.

To make doubly sure that he'd catch Amber, the
man placed a second trap on a nearby stump. He
knew that a wary fox would often perch on a rock or
a stump to study the bait. If a fox jumped on this
stump, the animal would land on the trap.

Before leaving, the trapper tied a piece of pink
tape to a tree branch so that it would be easy to find
the spot on his return. He'd already caught one fox
that morning, and he was confident that he'd get this
one too. When he reached his vehicle, he tossed the
empty canvas bag into the back. As well as the bag,

there were nine muskrats in the cargo box and the fox
he'd caught earlier that day. The dead fox was
Amber's brother, Snap.

●

That afternoon the wind dropped and the
temperature began to fall. When Amber set off at
dark, ice was already forming at the bottom of the
ditch. The young vixen had decided to leave the area.
She was certain the wolves would be back, and the
human who had watched her from the right-of-way
made her nervous. It was too dangerous for her to
stay.

She didn't dare travel on the embankment for fear
of the wolves. Instead, she followed the rail line
through the fields and bush. On the other side of the
bend, she noticed a pile of rocks. It was the sort of
place where she'd often found chipmunks and mice.
Because of the wolves, she hadn't eaten the previous
night, and she was hungry. She went over to
investigate the spot.

Carefully she tip-toed around the pile. Then she
jumped lightly onto the stones and sniffed among the
crevices. Her nose, sharpened by hunger, caught a
whiff of mouse scent between two boulders. From

where she stood, she could see that the earth had
been disturbed. A mouse had been buried there by
another fox.

The only way she could reach the spot was at
ground level. Jumping down from the rocks, she
circled the pile until she was opposite the opening
between the two boulders. Intent on getting the mouse,
she moved forward and stepped squarely on the trap.

Nothing happened.

The damp earth hiding the trap had frozen into a
hard shell. The moment Amber put her paw on the
frozen soil, she felt it shift under her weight. Startled,
she leapt back. Much as she wanted the mouse, she
realized something was wrong.

Cautiously she studied the ground around the
opening. One of the cocking levers, exposed by the
movement of the trap, gleamed in the moonlight.
Stretching her neck toward it, she detected a scent of
metal, a human odor.

Alarmed by her discovery, Amber hurried away from
the rock pile and continued on her journey. A few
hours later she decided to leave the rail line and strike
out in a new direction. Gazing up at the night sky, the
bright star Polaris caught her eye. She headed north.

CHAPTER TEN

WINTER

The countryside north of the rail line was dotted with small farms, woodlots, and pastures. Amber traveled cautiously, keeping to the edge of the farms, avoiding humans and dogs. Some days later she came to a vast forest. Rather than continuing into the woods, she headed east along its border.

The young vixen slept in the open, making use of high ground to watch for danger. As November progressed, the weather grew colder, stilling the waters and turning the ground to stone. One morning a nearby pond was covered with a thin layer of ice as clear as glass. When Amber bent down to take a drink, she bumped her nose on it.

The fox wasn't the only one to be fooled by the ice. While she was trying to puzzle out the situation, a pair of black ducks glided into the pond on curved wings. Instead of landing with a gentle splash on the water, the ducks slid across the frozen surface on their tails.

The following day, Amber ventured out onto the ice. Because it was so slippery she was timid at first, but she soon gained confidence. After managing a slow walk, she broke into a trot. When she tried to turn, she went into a long skid. Once she got over her fright, she found she enjoyed sliding on the ice. For the rest of the morning she played on the pond.

•

That night a halo around the moon warned of a change in the weather. Early the next morning it began to snow. The snow continued for most of the day. By the time the sky cleared, a thick white blanket covered the countryside.

Amber had curled up in a thicket during the storm, and had been warm and comfortable. Shaking the snow from her coat, she stepped out of her lair. To her surprise she sank up to her knees. She'd seen snow before, but only thin coatings of it. This snowfall was quite different. It was so deep it had smoothed the features of the landscape.

The young fox plodded through the snow looking for something to eat, but found nothing. Most of the birds had gone south. Woodchucks and chipmunks were hibernating in their dens, voles and mice were hidden in their tunnels under the snow, and muskrats were safe beneath the ice.

Winter, the season of hunger, had arrived.

Tired and hungry, Amber started back to her thicket. Just then three blue jays flashed by, calling, *Tool-ool! tool-ool!* She watched the gaudy birds disappear into the cedars — the first sign of life she'd seen all day. She'd only gone a little distance when she heard the jays shrieking in the cedar trees. Their high-pitched cries of alarm made her curious.

Quickly she retraced her steps. As soon as she entered the cedars, Amber saw the cause of the commotion. A sharp-shinned hawk had caught one of the blue jays and knocked it to the ground. The hawk was standing in the snow, clutching the dead bird while the other two jays circled overhead, screaming.

Amber's appearance drove the blue jays into an even greater frenzy. Alerted by the jays' change of tone, the hawk looked up and saw the fox. The hawk — who was hardly bigger than the jay — tried to fly away with his kill. But he couldn't lift it off the ground. At the last second the hawk gave up and escaped into a tree.

Ignoring the hawk, Amber claimed her prize. She was so hungry that she ate the jay without removing its feathers. The hawk glared at the fox in helpless rage, then flew off. When Amber had finished her meal, she licked a few blue feathers from her chops and headed back to the thicket.

•

Most wild creatures had taken shelter during the snowstorm. But as soon as it was over, they resumed their search for food. The next day Amber saw many footprints in the snow — from the deep, slotted holes of deer, to the lacy tracings of mice and voles. A little pile of fresh pine scales on the top of a stump revealed that a red squirrel had already been out to feed.

That afternoon Amber discovered the entrance to a mouse tunnel. The ribbon of scent coming from the hole made her drool. Inhaling the scent, she began to dig, expecting at any moment to uncover the mice. But the more she dug, the fainter became their odor. The mice were running down the tunnel ahead of her.

Instinctively she resorted to an age-old mousing tactic. At the next entrance, she circled the hole until she caught a whiff of mouse scent through the snow. Having locating the tunnel, she sat down and listened for the scrape of tiny feet. When a mouse came along, her sensitive ears pinpointed its position. Then she pounced, punching through the snow with both paws.

This type of hunting required a keen nose, super-sensitive ears, and quick reflexes. Amber was well equipped for the task. The first time she used the listen-and-pounce method, she caught more mice than she could eat. Remembering what her mother had taught her, she buried three mice in the snow. These she would eat later.

When she checked her larder the following day, the mice were gone. Prints in the snow revealed the culprits. One had been stolen by a raven, who had watched her bury it. The other two mice had been dug up by a weasel during the night. These losses taught Amber a lesson. From then on, she looked around before burying her prey, and removed the traces by smoothing the snow over their graves with her nose.

•

The young vixen also learned that once the snow came, hunting was best during the daylight hours. In winter the days were short and the nights were cold. Mice and voles, the main items of her diet, were more active in the daytime because the sun's warmth filtered through the snow and warmed their tunnels.

One afternoon, while she was listening by a mouse tunnel, a ruffed grouse flew past. Just before it went out of sight, Amber saw the bird suddenly swerve and plunge into a snowbank. The fox had never seen a grouse do this before, and she trotted over to investigate.

Powder snow was still sifting into the hole when she reached the spot. Curious to know what had happened to the bird, Amber poked her nose into the cavity. The grouse exploded in her face, showering